AF603943

**Notion press India pvt. ltd._Chennai, India**

**Notion press.com**

## DEDICATED TO

**"MOTHER FATHER AND NATURE**
**IS OUR FIRST TEACHER**
**SO**
**I DEDICAT THIS BOOK**
**TO NATURE AND ALL MY TEACHERS."**

**By - Sonakshi Sonje**

Notion press India pvt.ltd. Chennai,India

# JOURNEY OF LISA

## TERASURE HUNT

{PART 1}

By : Sonakshi Vijay Sonje
Pl-26, GT-1356, Faizpur, Tal-Yawal, Dist-Jalgaon
Maharashtra, India , 425503
Contact : 9422174811, 9422174805
E-mail : shinesonje82@gmail.com

**ISBN : 979-889133482-3**

**Publisher**

**Notionpress.com**

From : Chennai, India
Jointly Founded by Naveen Valasakumar, Jana Pillay
& Bhargava Adepally
Email ID: publish@notionpress.com.
Phone Number: +91 44 46315631.

***

First Edition : 09 October 2023
Front page & picture : Notion Press.com
Price : 150/Rs

Notion press India pvt.ltd. Chennai,India

# INDEX

## Writer's Note:

*While "The Enigmatic Expedition: Lisa's Treasure Hunt - First Series" may be described as a thrilling adventure filled with mystery and friendship, The narrative appears to follow a familiar pattern of a group of young friends embarking on a quest, encountering challenges, and ultimately learning valuable life lessons.*

*with Lisa being the inquisitive and courageous leader, and her friends each possessing conveniently unique skills for the quest. The presence of an enigmatic mentor guiding the group could be seen as a trope commonly used in adventure stories. Critics might also point out that the use of magic and enchanted forests in the plot may contribute to a sense of overused fantasy elements, potentially leaving some readers craving more innovation and a fresh perspective on the adventure genre.*

*In terms of writing style, some readers may find the vivid descriptions and intricate plot twists* overwhelming or overly dramatic, suggesting that the author relies on these elements rather than focusing on subtlety and nuance.

Overall, while the book may appeal to those who enjoy traditional adventure stories with a focus on friendship and self-discovery.

## About :

**This book is written by sonakshi sonje ,I am from india, this is the very creative and adventuraus book, from 4 to 15 years kids can read this book it teaches them about adventure, some morals, creativity and love about nature and animals.**

## Introduction :

Embark on a thrilling adventure with Lisa and her loyal friends as they unravel the mysteries of an ancient treasure in "The Enigmatic Expedition: Lisa's Treasure Hunt - First Series." This captivating tale takes readers on a heart-pounding journey filled with secrets, danger, and the power of friendship.

Lisa, an inquisitive and courageous young girl, stumbles upon an old map that leads to an unimaginable treasure hidden deep within an enchanted forest. Determined to uncover its secrets, Lisa gathers her closest friends, each possessing unique skills that prove vital in their quest.

As they venture into the unknown, the group encounters a series of puzzling riddles, cunning traps, and unexpected challenges. They must rely on their wits and bond as a team to overcome each obstacle they encounter. Throughout their journey, they discover that the treasure holds a profound significance, linked to a forgotten era and a forgotten people.

Guided by the wisdom of an enigmatic mentor, the friends learn valuable life lessons about trust, loyalty, and perseverance. Each member of the group faces personal trials that push them to their limits, testing the strength of their friendships and their individual character.

"The Enigmatic Expedition: Lisa's Treasure Hunt - First Series" is an enchanting blend of adventure, mystery, and self-discovery. With vivid descriptions, intricate plot twists, and a sprinkling of magic, this first installment in the series will leave readers eagerly turning the pages, yearning to unravel the secrets hidden within the ancient treasure.

Will Lisa and her friends succeed in their quest and unlock the treasure's true purpose? Join them as they navigate treacherous landscapes, solve perplexing riddles, and face unexpected adversaries in a race against time. Prepare to be captivated by this gripping tale of camaraderie and adventure, where the bonds of friendship prove to be the most valuable treasure of all.

"The Enigmatic Expedition: Lisa's Treasure Hunt - First Series" is an enthralling adventure that will appeal to readers of all ages, inviting them to believe in the power of friendship and the endless possibilities that lie within the unknown.

# 1. INTRODUCTOIN TO OUR FRIEND'S OF THIS JOURNEY

**Oh hi I am Lisa now you all that are reading my book they know what is the topic of my story. Ok first I introduce myself my name as you know Lisa. I really like to travel and when I want to achieve anything then.**

**I don't listen anyone for it. And you know that I am the best student in my school I love my all friends, teachers and of course my family. Oh hey! Mia come here what happened why are you crying ? ohho emmm Lisa my brother broke my best mug of tea in my life.**

**What! Only for this anyway hi this is my best friend Mia she was crying and crying everyday but you know what then also I like her because she was very kind and help me in every situation. { sound come from back } hi Lisa , hi Sophia.**

See this is my new hair belt but you cann't touch it because it is very expensive for you it is of 10 thousand. Oh yes, Lisa said. Ok bye Lisa Sophia said. Feww! Thank god she gone yes this is my one more friend Sophia you know! She was show me and my other friends of her expensive things like this hair belt. Oh what is going there let's go.

{ Emma's mother angry with her } Come here stop please stop come here Emma don't ran away. What happened aunty why are you angry with Emma, what is she do now?

Ohh Lisa everyday she trubble to others and they complain me of her action I really harass with her behaviour what should I do now? Emma's mother said.

Don't worry aunty I will try to explain her. This is my naughty friend everyday she trouble to us. But ever then we like her and accepted her our friend. And the last my very foodie friend she is Emily. Let's go to the Emily's house what are you doing Emily Lisa said. Nothing I am only eating my sweets that mom brought from sweets shop Emily said. { sound come from back }

**what! Emily's mother said. You eat all the sweets? No mom only just a few boxes. Oh my god it is not few Emily, I brought this sweets for guest and you eat all of this? Oh god what I do now don't worry aunty I have some boxes of sweets at home I will give you Lisa said. Thank you Lisa. Emily's mother said. Sorry mom! Emily said. These are my friends of my beautiful journey Okay bye...**

## 2. LET'S PLAY

**One day Lisa is watering her plants and yes Lisa also like gardening. Oh! Hi friends what happened why are you came here? Lisa, can you please come for playing in garden? Emily said. Ok ok but at first I had to complete my this work. Ok then we will wait for you and also help to you. Mia said. Come then take this and add it in the soil. But Lisa why this rotten fruits and vegetables are adding in the soil? Mia ask.**

**That's because when we add it in soil it fulfill the requirement of nutrients in the soil.{ after some time } few! Please now come for play oh yes wait a minutes I 'ill bring my badminton for play. Lisa said. Ohh! Yes come fast.**

**{Then they go to the playground for playing they play all over the day} friends now we had to go home because it is 7:30 of evening. Yes you are right Lisa we had to go home. Ok bye friends yes bye Lisa. Tomorrow we all are playing in my backyard. Ok Lisa we all are come to your home.**

**One sunny afternoon, Lisa invited her friends over to her house for a delightful day of fun and laughter. As they gathered in Lisa's**

backyard, they couldn't contain their excitement. The backyard was transformed into a magical wonderland with colorful balloons, streamers, and games scattered around. The air was filled with joyous giggles and the sweet aroma of freshly baked cookies, which Lisa's mom had prepared for them.

Eager to start their adventure, Lisa suggested they play a game of hide-and-seek. The friends scattered in different directions, their laughter echoing through the neighborhood as they searched for the perfect hiding spots. Mia found refuge behind a tall oak tree, while Sophia squeezed herself behind a blooming rose bush. Emma hid in the garden shed, and Emily cleverly climbed up a tree, camouflaging herself among the branches.

Lisa, being the seeker, closed her eyes and began counting. "1, 2, 3... ready or not, here I come!" she exclaimed. Lisa searched high and low, peeking behind every corner, determined to find her friends. Mia, Sophia, Emma, and Emily held their breath, trying their best not to give away their hiding places.

**Soon enough, Lisa's keen eyes spotted a glimpse of Mia's colorful dress peeping out from behind the oak tree.**

**Mia couldn't help but burst into laughter as Lisa triumphantly found her. They high-fived and continued the search.Sophia was the next to be discovered, as her giggles betrayed her hiding spot. Lisa reached out to Sophia, who emerged from behind the rose bush, her face flushed with excitement.As Lisa moved closer to finding the remaining two, she could hear a faint rustling sound coming from the garden shed. With a mischievous grin, Lisa threw open the**

**shed doors, revealing Emma sitting among gardening tools and pots. Emma erupted into laughter, and the trio joined forces to find the final hiding spot.**

**They ventured toward the towering tree, scanning its branches. Lisa tilted her head and squinted her eyes, trying to distinguish between the leaves and her friend. Suddenly, a small giggle gave Emily away, and Lisa spotted her perched on a sturdy branch, her legs dangling playfully.**

**With everyone found, the group rejoiced, cheering and clapping. They were all winners in their own right, having shared a delightful game of hide-and-seek filled with joy and friendly competition.**

**As the sun began to set, casting a warm orange glow across the sky, Lisa and her friends gathered on a cozy blanket spread out on the grass.**

**They indulged in the delicious cookies Lisa's mom had baked, sharing stories, dreams, and plans for their next adventure. With hearts full of happiness and cherished memories, Lisa, Mia, Sophia, Emma, and Emily knew that their friendship was a bond that would last a lifetime. They vowed to support each.**

**other through thick and thin, and to keep the spirit of playfulness alive in their hearts forever. As the evening came to a close, the friends bid each other**

**goodbye, promising to meet again soon. They went home with wide smiles on their faces, knowing that the magical bond they shared would always bring them back together for more wonderful adventures.**

**And so, Lisa and her friends, Mia, Sophia, Emma, and Emily, continued to create lifelong memories, their friendship growing stronger with each passing days.**

## 3. EMPTY BOWL

Lisa, Emma, Emily, and Mia were inseparable and always found joy in each other's company. One sunny afternoon, they decided to explore the nearby forest.

As they walked deeper into the woods, they stumbled upon a peculiar sight—a tiny, hungry cat meowing pitifully beside an empty bowl. Its eyes were filled with longing, and the girls couldn't bear to see it in such distress. Moved by the cat's plight, Lisa, Emma, Emily, and Mia exchanged concerned glances. Sophia, the youngest among them, had been trailing behind, but her heart swelled with empathy when she saw her friends' faces.

"I can't stand to see the poor little thing go hungry," Lisa said, her voice filled with compassion. Emma nodded in agreement. "We should find some food for it. Maybe there's a nearby farm where we can get some milk." Emily, the resourceful one, had an idea.

" I remember passing a farmer's market on our way here. They might have some leftovers that they'd be willing to give us." Mia, the optimist, chimed in, "Let's split up and search for food.

We'll find something to fill that empty bowl in no time!" With renewed determination, the four friends dispersed in different directions. Lisa and Mia headed towards the farmer's market, while Emma and Emily ventured towards the nearby As they scoured the market, Lisa and Mia explained their mission to the vendors.

Touched by the girls' kindness, the vendors gladly provided them. Meanwhile, Emma and Emily visited several farms, explaining their quest to the farmers. One farmer, Mr. Johnson, was deeply moved by their intentions. He filled a basket with freshly laid eggs and a bowl of warm milk from his own cow, promising to check on the cat once they returned. Excitedly, Emma and Emily rushed back to the woods, eager to reunite with their friends and the little cat. Sophia, who had been patiently waiting with the cat, was overjoyed to see her friends return with food.

The four friends gathered around the empty bowl, placing the vegetables, milk, and eggs inside. The little cat, sensing their kindness, purred and began to eat heartily. Its tiny whiskers twitched with delight as it devoured the much-needed nourishment.

**Tears welled up in Lisa's eyes as she watched the little cat eat. "Look at how happy it is! We made a difference today." Emma smiled warmly, her heart brimming with pride.**

**"Together, we can do amazing things. No bowl should ever stay empty when we're around." The friends sat in a circle, sharing stories and laughter as the little cat nestled contentedly among them.**

**They realized that this experience had strengthened their bond and taught them the power of compassion and teamwork. From that day forward, Lisa, Emma, Emily, Mia, Sophia, and the little cat became inseparable companions. They continued their adventures.**

# 4. WHAT IS INSITE THE GROUND

Once upon a sunny day, Lisa, Emma, Emily, Sophia, and Mia gathered at their favorite playground. The vibrant swings, towering slides, and bouncy seesaws beckoned them to embark on a playful adventure. Little did they know that beneath their feet, buried deep in the ground, a mysterious secret awaited their discovery.

As the friends raced around the playground, laughing and playing, they stumbled upon an ancient-looking map lying near the sandbox.

Curiosity sparked within their hearts, and they huddled together, examining the faded parchment. It depicted a hidden treasure buried underground, waiting to be found.

Excitement tingled in the air as Lisa, the group's natural leader, suggested they follow the map's clues and embark on a real-life treasure hunt. With unanimous agreement, the friends set off, their youthful spirits filled with anticipation.

The first clue led them to a tree near the edge of the playground. Underneath a particular branch, they uncovered a small shovel engraved with the

**name "Emma." Intrigued, they realized that each clue was personalized for one of them. Holding the shovel, Emma grinned and eagerly led the way.**

**Next, they followed the map to a spot near the swings. Sophia, being the tallest of the group, was instructed to reach for something hidden among the leaves.**

**As she stretched her hand out, she pulled out a metal keychain with the name "Emily" etched on it. Each step of the treasure hunt felt more magical than the last.**

**Mia, with her keen sense of observation, discovered a hidden compartment beneath the merry-go-round. Inside, there was a small box labeled "Sophia." Excitement coursed through the group as Sophia opened it to reveal a shiny brass key. With the key in hand, they followed the map to a precise location near the climbing wall. As they unlocked a hidden door on the wall, the friends were met with a tunnel that led underground. Braving the darkness, they ventured forth, feeling the cool air enveloping them.**

The tunnel led to a vast underground chamber filled with glittering jewels and ancient artifacts. It was a treasure trove beyond their wildest dreams. Amidst their astonishment, they realized that the treasure wasn't material wealth but the bond they shared as friends and the joy they found in their adventures. Laughing and celebrating, the friends collected a few mementos from the chamber to remember their remarkable discovery.

With the map and their hearts full, they made their way back to the playground, emerging from the secret tunnel. As they reemerged into the sunlight, they couldn't help but be grateful for their playful spirits and the unexpected journey they had embarked upon. Hand in hand, Lisa, Emma, Emily, Sophia, and Mia returned.

## 5. WHAT IS INSITE THE TREASURI

**On a sunny summer morning, five best friends, Lisa, Emma, Emily, Mia, and Sophia, gathered at Lisa's house with excitement gleaming in their eyes. They had been planning a grand adventure for weeks, and today was the day they were going to embark on their treasure hunt.**

**Lisa, being the adventurous and curious one, had stumbled upon an old map while cleaning her attic. The map seemed to lead to a hidden treasure buried somewhere in the nearby forest. Unable to contain her excitement, she immediately called her friends and shared the exciting news.**

**As the girls gathered in Lisa's living room, they knew that their treasure hunt would require careful planning and preparation. Sophia, the organized and practical thinker, suggested that they first seek permission from their parents and pack essential items in their backpacks.**

**With determination in their hearts, they approached their parents one by one, explaining their ambitious plan and asking for permission. Each parent, though initially apprehensive, was**

**convinced by the girls' enthusiasm and gave their blessing.**

**They emphasized the importance of safety, caution, and staying together throughout their adventure.**

**Now armed with parental permission and excited anticipation, the girls rushed to gather their backpacks and pack them with the necessary supplies.**

**They meticulously packed water bottles, snacks, flashlights, extra batteries, a compass, and a first-aid kit. They wanted to be fully prepared for any obstacle they might encounter on their quest for the hidden treasure.**

**Once their backpacks were ready, the girls huddled together around the old map. It was tattered and faded, with markings indicating a path deep into the forest.**

**The excitement grew stronger as they studied the map, tracing their fingers over the mysterious symbols and deciphering clues that would lead them to the treasure.**

**Before they set off, Mia, the resourceful and imaginative one, suggested they create a plan of action.**

**They divided the tasks among themselves: Lisa would navigate using the compass, Emma would keep a lookout for any potential dangers, Emily would document their adventure through photographs, Mia would use her artistic skills to sketch the surroundings, and Sophia would ensure they stayed on track with the map.**

**With their roles assigned, the girls made their way to the edge of the forest.**

**The trees stood tall, their leaves whispering in the gentle breeze. As they took their first steps into the dense foliage, a sense of wonder and anticipation filled the air. The adventure awaited them, and they were ready to embark on a journey that would test their friendship, courage, and problem-solving skills.**

**They had their backpacks filled with supplies, parents' permission, and the map leading them to a hidden treasure. The five friends stepped into the unknown, ready to unravel the secrets of the forest**

and discover the priceless treasure that lay hidden within.

Little did they know that their lives were about to be forever changed by the experiences that awaited them in the heart of the forest. As the girls ventured deeper into the forest, the surroundings began to transform. Sunlight filtered through the dense canopy, casting a mystical glow on the path ahead. The air carried the scent of wildflowers and earth, creating an enchanting atmosphere.

With every step, the girls became more engrossed in the beauty and mystery of their surroundings. Mia couldn't resist stopping every now and then to capture the vibrant colors of flowers and the intricate patterns of tree bark in her sketches. Emily eagerly documented these moments with her camera, ensuring that every memory was preserved.

Sophia diligently compared the landmarks on the map with the actual surroundings, making sure they stayed on the right track. Lisa skillfully guided the group, occasionally pausing to study the compass and confirm their direction. Emma kept a watchful eye, alert for any signs of danger or unexpected obstacles along the way.

As they continued deeper into the forest, the girls began to encounter challenges that tested their problem-solving skills. They encountered a roaring river blocking their path, and after a brief discussion, they decided to build a makeshift bridge using fallen tree branches.

With teamwork and determination, they successfully crossed the rushing water and continued on their quest. The forest seemed to come alive around them, with the sounds of chirping birds and rustling leaves filling their ears.

They marveled at the sight of a family of deer grazing peacefully in a nearby clearing, their presence adding to the magical ambiance of their adventure. Hours turned into a day, and the girls pressed on, their excitement undiminished. As the sun began to dip below the horizon, casting long shadows over the forest, they knew it was time to find a suitable campsite for the night. Following a small clearing, they discovered a cozy spot surrounded by ancient trees, providing a sense of security and tranquility.

They carefully set up their tents and started a campfire, its warm glow illuminating their faces as they shared stories and laughter. Over a simple meal of sandwiches and snacks from their backpacks, they discussed their progress and speculated about the nature of the treasure they sought. As the night sky adorned itself with countless stars, their eyes filled with wonder.

They felt a connection to something greater than themselves, as if the forest itself held the answers they sought. In the quiet stillness, they made a pact to continue their search for the treasure with unwavering determination and unwavering friendship.

With their hearts filled with anticipation and dreams of what lay ahead, the girls eventually retired to their tents, exhausted but eager for the adventures of the following day.

They fell asleep under a starry sky, their minds buzzing with excitement, knowing that the true magic of their journey was only just beginning.

They fell asleep under a starry sky, their minds buzzing with excitement, knowing that the true magic of their journey was only just beginning. Little did they know that the forest held more secrets than they could have ever imagined.

As they slept, the forest whispered ancient tales and guarded the treasure they sought, waiting for the girls to unravel its mysteries in the days to come.

# 6. PIRATE'S COVE

**Lisa, Emma, Emily, Mia, and Sophia stood at the edge of the sparkling sea, gazing out at the mysterious Pirate's Cove. Legends whispered of hidden treasures buried deep within the sandy shores, waiting to be discovered by brave adventurers. Excitement filled the air as the friends clutched a worn-out map they had stumbled upon in the attic of an old bookstore. The map seemed to be a key to unlocking the secrets of Pirate's Cove. It depicted a series of landmarks and hidden clues that would guide them to the long-lost treasure. Eager to embark on their quest, the friends huddled together around the map, tracing their fingers along its faded lines. Lisa, the natural leader of the group, studied the map intently, deciphering the first clue.**

**"According to the map," Lisa exclaimed, "we must follow the old lighthouse's beam until we reach the giant palm tree on the eastern shore." With a sense of adventure pulsing through their veins, the friends set off on their quest, marching along the sandy beach towards the looming lighthouse. As they walked, they laughed, sharing stories and imagining the treasures they might find.**

**After what felt like an eternity, they reached the lighthouse. Its weathered stone walls stood tall against the crashing waves. As the sun began to set, casting a warm golden glow over the horizon, the lighthouse's beam shot into the sky, guiding their way. With the beam as their guiding light, the friends followed its path, weaving through tall grasses and over rocky terrain. They ventured deeper into Pirate's Cove, the salty ocean breeze guiding their steps. Just as the map had indicated, they reached the giant palm tree, standing tall and proud.**

**"This must be the spot," Mia exclaimed, her eyes widening with anticipation. Emily, the most nimble of the group, climbed up the palm tree, her gaze fixed on the horizon. She spotted a peculiar rock formation in the distance and called out, "I see it! The next clue lies within the Cave of Whispers!" The friends eagerly made their way towards the intriguing cave, their footsteps quickening with each passing moment. As they approached, the sounds of crashing waves transformed into hushed whispers, echoing through the cavernous entrance. Their hearts raced as they ventured into the dark abyss, their flashlights piercing through the gloom.**

**The cave walls seemed to breathe with secrets, and the friends felt the weight of history pressing upon them. Suddenly, a gust of wind swept through the cave, extinguishing their flashlights. In the darkness, their voices trembled with fear, but they clung to each other, finding comfort in their friendship. With the help of their map and the dim glow of moonlight filtering through cracks in the cave's ceiling, they managed to find a hidden passage. Braving the unknown, they cautiously followed it, their anticipation growing with each step.**

**Little did they know that their journey was just beginning. The treasures of Pirate's Cove awaited them, and as their footsteps echoed through the depths of the cave, they could sense that their lives were about to change forever.**

**As the friends pressed onward through the hidden passage, their hearts filled with a mixture of excitement and trepidation. The narrow path twisted and turned, leading them deeper.**

**into the heart of the cave. Drips of water echoed in the darkness, adding an eerie soundtrack to their adventure. After what seemed like an eternity, they emerged into a vast chamber adorned with stalactites and stalagmites, shimmering like diamonds in the faint light. The air was thick with anticipation as they surveyed their surroundings, searching for the next clue.**

**Sophia's sharp eyes caught sight of an ancient carving etched into the rocky wall. It depicted a ship sailing towards a rising sun.**

**"Look, everyone!" she exclaimed. "The map shows this carving. It must be the key to our next destination!"**

## 7. ENCHANTED FOREST

**(Their next destination would be the enchanted forest)**

**With their backpacks filled with supplies and hearts brimming with excitement, the five girls set off on a beautiful trail that led them deeper into the dense forest.**

**As they ventured further, the air became crisp, and the songs of birds echoed through the tall, ancient trees. The sunlight filtered through the thick foliage, casting an ethereal glow on the forest floor.**

**They followed a winding path, which seemed to guide them deeper into the heart of the enchanted forest. The forest hummed with an otherworldly energy, filling the girls with a sense of anticipation. Suddenly, they stumbled upon a clearing, where a babbling brook cascaded over rocks, and vibrant flowers painted the landscape in a myriad of colors.**

**As they approached the brook, Sophia noticed a shimmering light emanating from a nearby tree.**

Curiosity piqued, the girls followed Sophia towards the tree, their eyes widening in awe.

The tree trunk seemed to be carved with intricate symbols, and at its base, there was a keyhole. Sophia produced a small, ornate key from her pocket and carefully inserted it into the keyhole.

To their amazement, the tree trunk began to creak open, revealing a hidden passageway beyond. The girls exchanged glances filled with excitement and stepped into the unknown.

They found themselves in a breathtaking glen, where the soft glow of fireflies illuminated the air. Trees stretched upward like ancient sentinels, and a gentle breeze whispered secrets of the forest.

As they wandered deeper into the glen, the girls encountered various magical creatures. They witnessed graceful fairies flitting among the flowers, mischievous pixies playing pranks, and wise old owls hooting from the treetops.

The forest seemed to respond to their presence, enchanting them with its beauty and filling their hearts with a deep sense of wonder.

Their exploration led them to a magical waterfall that shimmered with a rainbow cascade. The girls couldn't resist the urge to dip their toes into the crystal-clear water.

As they did, the water seemed to possess a revitalizing energy, washing away any worries or doubts that may have lingered within them.

They felt an indescribable connection with the enchanted forest, as if they had found a place where dreams came alive. As dusk approached, the girls decided to rest near the waterfall, surrounded by the soft sounds of nature.

They shared stories, laughter, and dreams under the twinkling stars, grateful for the bonds they had forged and the magical journey they had embarked upon. Little did they know, their adventure in the enchanted forest was only just beginning.

The forest held countless secrets and mysteries, waiting to be discovered.

With hearts full of anticipation, Lisa, Emma, Emily, Mia, and Sophia drifted off to sleep, eagerly awaiting the dawn of a new day, eager to unravel the wonders that awaited them in the enchanted forest.

As the first rays of sunlight filtered through the leaves, the girls awoke to the symphony of birdsong.

Excitement filled their hearts as they prepared to continue their exploration of the enchanted forest. Sophia, with her innate sense of adventure, suggested they follow a narrow trail that led deeper into the woods.

The path wound through a dense thicket, adorned with delicate flowers and vibrant moss-covered rocks. It seemed as if the forest itself was leading them onward, guiding them to the heart of its secrets. As they walked, a soft, melodic humming reached their ears, growing louder with each step.

They followed the enchanting melody, which led them to a glade bathed in dappled sunlight. In the center stood a towering ancient tree, its branches spreading like a protective canopy. Curiosity danced in their eyes as they approached, drawn by the irresistible allure of the music.

As they neared the tree, the girls gasped in awe. Its trunk was adorned with colorful ribbons, fluttering in the gentle breeze. Mia reached out, her fingers grazing the ribbons, and a warm energy surged through her, sending tingles up her spine. Intrigued, the others followed suit, each experiencing their own surge of magic.

Unbeknownst to the girls, their touch had awakened the spirit of the tree—a graceful being known as Elara. With a soft voice, she greeted them, revealing herself as the guardian of the enchanted forest. Elara explained that the ribbons on the tree represented the dreams and wishes of those who had ventured into the forest before them.

Moved by their presence, Elara invited the girls to tie their own ribbons onto the tree, symbolizing their deepest desires.

**Lisa wished for courage to follow her dreams, Emma yearned for creativity to blossom, Emily sought wisdom to guide her path, Mia longed for a compassionate heart, and Sophia desired a connection to the natural world.**

**As they tied their ribbons, a gentle magic spread through their fingertips, carrying their intentions to the heart of the forest.**

**The girls felt a profound sense of unity, knowing that they were not alone in their dreams, but supported by the very essence of the enchanted forest.**

**Elara then shared that she had a gift for each of them, a token of the forest's gratitude for their respect and love.**

**From a hidden hollow beneath her roots, she produced small vials filled with glowing, iridescent dust.**

**As they accepted the gifts, Elara whispered that the dust held the power to amplify their innate qualities and strengths.**

Filled with a renewed sense of purpose and determination, the girls bid farewell to Elara and continued their journey through the enchanted forest.

With each step, they grew more attuned to the subtle magic that surrounded them, discovering hidden wonders and encountering mystical creatures along the way.

# 8. JUNGAL SAFARI

**A land surrounded by lush greenery and teeming with wildlife, there were six adventurous friends named Lisa, Emma, Emily, Mia, Sophia, and their trusty canine companion, Treasure.**

**They were all avid explorers and had a deep love for nature. Their latest expedition led them to embark on a thrilling jungle safari, brimming with excitement and the promise of discovery.**

**The sun rose high in the sky as the group gathered at the entrance of the dense jungle. Lisa, the brave and determined leader, shared the map she had meticulously studied, outlining their route through the wilderness.**

**The friends eagerly listened, their hearts pounding with anticipation. Their first challenge was to locate a hidden treasure deep within the heart of the jungle.**

**They had heard tales of a lost artifact said to possess mystical powers and bring good fortune to anyone who found it. Excitement filled the air as they set off on their treasure hunt, following the faint clues left behind by ancient explorers.**

Underneath the towering canopy, the friends maneuvered through thick foliage and tangled vines, their senses heightened by the exotic sounds and scents surrounding them.

The forest floor crackled with every step, and the chirping of birds echoed through the trees, creating a symphony of nature. Mia, with her keen eye for detail, noticed peculiar markings on the bark of a giant tree. She called the others over, and they all examined the engravings closely.

It was a riddle, leading them to a hidden cave concealed behind a cascading waterfall.

Excitedly, the friends made their way through the glistening curtain of water, their hearts pounding with the thrill of the unknown. Inside the cave, they discovered a series of intricate puzzles and tests that challenged their wit and teamwork.

They encouraged each other, solving the riddles one by one, their laughter resonating through the caverns. As they approached the final puzzle, Sophia's knowledge of ancient hieroglyphics came to the fore.

She deciphered the code, revealing the exact location of the treasure. With renewed determination, they followed the path indicated, their footsteps leading them deeper into the jungle.

The sun began its descent, casting golden hues across the canopy, as the friends reached a clearing bathed in soft, ethereal light. Before them stood a magnificent ancient temple, its weathered stones telling stories of long-forgotten civilizations.

They knew their prize lay within. With bated breath, they stepped into the temple, awestruck by its grandeur. The air felt heavy with anticipation as they ventured further into its mysterious depths. Finally, in a chamber adorned with ornate carvings, they found it.

**But it was only the second clue it is watch then Lisa said "what is the meaning of this watch ? if we cann't find its meaning we connot go to our home." Suddenly Mia was started crying she said oh what! now we cannot go to our home emm! Mamma sss Dady sss. Don't worry we can found the answer of it.**

# 9. WILD WEST QUEST

And they reach here After their long and exhilarating adventure in the depths of the jungle safari, Lisa, Emma, Emily, Mia, and Sophia found themselves yearning for another thrilling escapade.

Eager to satiate their craving for excitement, they decided to embark on a daring quest to the Wild West. With their hearts filled with anticipation and a sense of adventure, the group gathered their belongings and set off on their journey.

As they rode on horseback through vast plains and towering mountains, the friends marveled at the stunning landscapes surrounding them. The endless expanse of the Wild West seemed to stretch as far as the eye could see, promising untold mysteries and treasures waiting to be discovered.

Their first stop was a small town named Dusty Creek. The dusty streets were lined with old wooden buildings, their facades weathered by time. The townsfolk, clad in worn-out boots and wide-brimmed hats, greeted the group with curious glances as they made their way to the local saloon.

Inside the dimly lit establishment, the friends overheard whispers of a legendary treasure hidden deep within the treacherous Badlands.

The tales spoke of riches beyond imagination, guarded by fierce outlaws and protected by perilous traps. Lisa, the fearless leader of the group, knew that this was the perfect opportunity for their wild west adventure to truly begin.

With renewed determination, Lisa, Emma, Emily, Mia, and Sophia set out towards the Badlands, their hearts brimming with a mix of excitement and apprehension.

The scorching sun beat down on them as they traversed the unforgiving desert, their horses galloping through the sandy terrain.

As they ventured deeper into the Badlands, the landscape grew increasingly rugged and unforgiving. The group encountered numerous challenges along the way, from treacherous ravines to deadly quicksand pits. Yet, their unwavering camaraderie and indomitable spirits carried them through each obstacle they faced.

One evening, as the sun began to set, they stumbled upon a hidden campsite. The flickering flames of a campfire danced in the twilight, casting eerie shadows against the rocky cliffs. A lone figure emerged from the darkness, his silhouette outlined by the dying embers.

Introducing himself as Sam, a seasoned cowboy with a twinkle in his eye, he revealed that he had been searching for the same treasure they sought.

Sam had spent years deciphering cryptic clues and braving the perils of the Badlands. Recognizing their shared goal and impressed by their determination, he offered his guidance to the group.

Together, the newfound alliance delved deeper into the treacherous Badlands, navigating labyrinthine canyons and scaling towering cliffs. They faced off against ruthless outlaws, engaging in thrilling shootouts that echoed through the arid desert air.

As they came closer to their destination, the group could almost taste the triumph. The final hurdle standing between them and the fabled treasure was a massive canyon, its depths shrouded in mystery.

With their hearts pounding, they devised a daring plan to cross the treacherous gorge and finally reach their prize.

As the sun rose on the following day, casting a golden glow over the vast canyon, the friends took a leap of faith. One by one, they swung on ropes and catapulted themselves across the abyss.

Cheers of triumph filled the air as they landed safely on the other side, a mere stone's throw away from the hidden treasure.

Their wild west quest had brought them to the brink of success, but what awaited them beyond the canyon's edge remained a mystery.

**With their spirits soaring and their determination unwavering, Lisa, Emma, Emily, Mia, Sophia, and Sam stood ready to face whatever challenges lay ahead in their pursuit of the legendary Wild West.**

# 10. NEW FRIEND COWBOY PITER

As Lisa, Emma, Emily, Mia, Sophia, and Sam stood on the edge of the canyon, catching their breath after their daring leap, they were greeted by a friendly voice. "Well, howdy there, folks! Mighty impressive jump y'all just made," said a man with a wide smile, stepping forward to join them.

Introducing himself as Peter, a seasoned cowboy and the owner of a nearby ranch, he extended a welcoming hand to the weary adventurers. "Y'all must be plum tuckered out from your journey. Why don't you come rest up at my humble abode? It's not too far from here."

Grateful for the offer of respite, the group gladly accepted Peter's invitation. They followed him as he led the way through the rugged terrain, gradually descending from the canyon towards the sprawling prairie where his ranch awaited.

The ranch, nestled amidst rolling hills and tall grass, exuded a sense of tranquility. Rustic wooden fences enclosed pastures dotted with horses, and the sound of gentle neighs filled the air. The group felt an immediate sense of calm wash over them as they approached the homestead.

Peter's home, a quaint yet cozy cabin, emanated warmth and hospitality. As they entered, they were greeted by the inviting aroma of freshly brewed coffee and homemade pie. The weary adventurers sank into comfortable armchairs, their tired muscles grateful for the chance to rest.

Over steaming mugs of coffee and plates piled high with pie, Peter regaled them with stories of his own adventures in the Wild West. He spoke of daring encounters with outlaws, treacherous rides through vast canyons, and the hidden treasures he had discovered along the way.

In turn, Lisa, Emma, Emily, Mia, and Sophia shared their own tales of the jungle safari and their quest to reach the Wild West. They recounted the challenges they had faced, the camaraderie that had kept them going, and their unwavering determination to uncover the legendary treasure.

As the evening wore on, the group found solace in the company of Peter and each other. They laughed, exchanged jokes, and reveled in the shared sense of adventure that had brought them together. It was a night filled with warmth, friendship, and the promise of even greater discoveries on the horizon.

The following morning, as the sun painted the sky with hues of orange and gold, Lisa, Emma, Emily, Mia, Sophia, Sam, and Peter gathered outside the cabin, ready to continue their quest. They knew that time was of the essence, and the legendary Wild West treasure awaited them.

With renewed energy and the support of their newfound friend, Peter, the adventurers set out once again. They bid farewell to the peaceful ranch and ventured deeper into the untamed wilderness of the Wild West, their hearts brimming with anticipation for the challenges and triumphs that lay ahead.

Together, they would face ruthless outlaws, conquer treacherous terrain, and uncover the secrets of the fabled treasure.

The bonds they had forged and the strength of their spirits would guide them through every trial they encountered, as they blazed a trail through the storied land of the Wild West.

And so, with determination in their hearts and the spirit of adventure coursing through their veins, Lisa, Emma, Emily, Mia, Sophia, Sam, and Peter pressed on, ready to create a legend of their own in the untamed frontier of the Wild West.

The journey through the Wild West continued, with Lisa, Emma, Emily, Mia, Sophia, Sam, and Peter facing new challenges at every turn. Together, they formed an unstoppable team, relying on their individual strengths and unwavering determination to overcome the obstacles that lay ahead.

Their path led them through vast canyons, where they skillfully maneuvered along narrow ledges and braved dizzying heights. They rode across open plains, their horses galloping with fierce determination, as the wind whipped through their hair and the dust kicked up beneath their hooves.

Along the way, they encountered remnants of abandoned mining towns, their dilapidated structures standing as silent witnesses to the past.

They explored eerie ghost towns, where whispers of forgotten stories seemed to echo through the empty streets. Yet, their focus remained unwavering on the fabled treasure that awaited them.Guided by the cryptic clues they had gathered and Peter's vast knowledge of the region, they gradually pieced together the puzzle leading to the hidden riches.

Each clue they deciphered brought them closer to their goal, and anticipation surged through their veins.

Their journey was not without its dangers. They encountered fierce outlaws who stood in their way, engaging in thrilling shootouts that tested their mettle and quick reflexes.

**With each victorious battle, they grew stronger and more united, forging an unbreakable bond as they faced the perils of the Wild West together.**

# 11. LOST MAP

**As Lisa, Emma, Emily, Mia, Sophia, Sam, and Peter ventured deeper into the Wild West, their quest for the legendary treasure faced a sudden setback.**

**While navigating through a treacherous ravine, they realized that they had lost their map—an essential guide to uncovering the location of the hidden riches. Anxiety crept into their hearts as they retraced their steps, scouring the rugged terrain in search of the missing map.**

**The vastness of the Wild West seemed to conspire against them, offering no clue as to where their precious guide might have disappeared.**

**Just as frustration threatened to overtake them, a glimmer of hope emerged from an unexpected source. Mia, with her keen eyes for detail, spotted a torn piece of parchment caught on a thorny bush.**

**They rushed towards it, their hearts pounding with anticipation. As they carefully pieced the torn fragments together, a sense of excitement washed over them. It was indeed a part of their lost map,**

revealing a crucial clue that would lead them closer to the fabled treasure.

Renewed determination filled their spirits, and they pressed on with unwavering resolve. Following the newly discovered clue, they embarked on a series of daring adventures.

They rode through vast desert landscapes, traversed treacherous canyons, and braved the unrelenting heat of the Wild West sun.

Each step brought them closer to their ultimate goal, their spirits unwavering despite the challenges they faced. Guided by their instincts and the fragments of the map, they encountered various obstacles and tests along the way.

They solved riddles, deciphered cryptic symbols, and navigated through hidden passages. The journey not only tested their physical prowess but also their wit and resilience.

Through it all, their bond grew stronger, fortified by the shared experiences and the unwavering support they offered one another. The Wild West had become more than just a backdrop for their adventure—it had become the crucible in which their characters were forged.

As they ventured deeper into uncharted territories, they discovered hidden oases and sacred Native American sites. They met wise old shamans who shared ancient wisdom, providing guidance and insight into the secrets of the land they traversed.

At long last, after overcoming countless challenges and obstacles, they stood at the entrance of a sacred valley—a place whispered about in legends.

The air crackled with anticipation as they entered the hallowed grounds, their steps slow and deliberate. In the heart of the valley, they discovered a hidden chamber—a chamber adorned with glittering jewels and precious metals.

The fabled treasure had finally been found. As they gazed upon its magnificence, a profound realization dawned upon them.

The true treasure was not the material wealth that lay before them. It was the journey itself—the bonds they had formed, the lessons they had learned, and the personal growth they had experienced along the way.

**The treasure was a testament to their unwavering spirit, their courage, and their unwavering belief in the power of friendship.**

**With gratitude in their hearts, they collected a small portion of the treasure—a token of their remarkable journey.**

**The rest would remain in ts sacred resting place, preserved for future adventurers to discover and cherish.**

**As they made their way back from the valley, their spirits soared. They carried with them not only the physical remnants of the treasure but also a profound sense of fulfillment and accomplishment. The Wild West had tested them, but it had also transformed them.**

**Together, they returned to Peter's ranch, where they celebrated their triumph. Amidst laughter, stories, and a shared sense of wonder, they knew that their adventure in the Wild West had changed their lives forever.**

**And so, as the sun set on their extraordinary quest, Lisa, Emma, Emily, Mia, Sophia, Sam, and Peter knew that their journey was far from over. The**

Wild West had imprinted itself upon their souls, leaving an indelible mark that would forever guide their future adventures.

United by the memories they had created and the lessons they had learned, they embraced the unknown, ready to embark on new quests and explore uncharted territories.

With the Wild West as their foundation, they stepped into the horizon, eager to create their own legends and inspire others to embrace the spirit of adventure.

And as they rode into the sunset, their hearts filled with gratitude and anticipation, they knew that the spirit of the Wild West would forever be a part of their untamed souls.

They traveled to distant lands, from the rugged peaks of the Himalayas to the dense jungles of the Amazon. Each new destination brought its own challenges and wonders, but their experiences in the Wild West had prepared them for whatever lay ahead. Their reputation as intrepid adventurers grew, and they became sought-after companions for those seeking to embark on their own extraordinary quests.

Together, they formed a society dedicated to exploration and the preservation of the world's natural and cultural treasures.The society, known as the Frontier Explorers, attracted individuals from all walks of life—brave souls who shared a common yearning for adventure and a deep respect for the beauty and diversity of the world.

Through their collective efforts, they sought to protect endangered environments, promote sustainable practices, and uncover the mysteries that lay hidden in every corner of the globe.

Under Lisa's leadership, the Frontier Explorers became a beacon of hope, inspiring others to embrace the spirit of adventure and stewardship. They organized expeditions to remote and endangered locations, working hand in hand with local communities to conserve the land and empower its people.

**Emma's expertise in horsemanship became invaluable, as she not only trained but the problems are not solve now they only got the answer of second clue but also one more big danger was coming soon in the journey of Lisa and her friends. It is oh! Not now it is in next topic. Ok bye.**

# 12. SCARY CAVE MONSTER

**As Lisa, Emma, Emily, Mia, Sophia, Sam, and Peter arrived in the peaceful village, a sense of unease hung in the air.**

**The villagers whispered of a terrifying cave monster that had recently emerged from the depths, wreaking havoc on their once tranquil lives.**

**Curiosity piqued, the adventurers sought out the village elder, who shared a harrowing tale of the creature's wrath.**

**The elder spoke of its immense size and ferocious nature, describing it as a fearsome guardian protecting a hidden secret deep within the cave.**

**Intrigued by the connection between the cave and their quest, Lisa, with her natural leadership, proposed a plan. They would confront the cave monster and uncover the truth it guarded. With their hearts set on solving the mystery, they ventured toward the forbidding entrance of the cave.**

Inside the dark and eerie cavern, the group moved cautiously, their footsteps echoing against the cold stone walls.

Suddenly, a guttural growl reverberated through the chamber, and a pair of glowing red eyes pierced the darkness.

The cave monster had appeared. Its massive form, covered in matted fur and sharp, gnarled claws, struck fear into their hearts. However, instead of attacking, the monster surprisingly began to communicate in a raspy, gravelly voice.

"I am the guardian of the cave," it spoke, its voice filled with an otherworldly resonance. "You seek the next clue, and I hold the answer within me."

Baffled yet intrigued, the group listened intently as the cave monster revealed that the key to unlocking the next clue lay in a clock. With each word, the mysterious puzzle began to unravel.

Realization dawned upon them. They recalled a clock mentioned in the tales of the legendary treasure, hidden in a long-abandoned town not far from the village.

They understood that this clock held the answers they sought, a vital piece of the puzzle that would lead them closer to their ultimate goal.

Thanking the cave monster for its cryptic revelation, they cautiously made their way out of the cavern, their minds racing with thoughts of the clock and the hidden secret it held. Determined and resolute, they set their sights on the forgotten town, ready to face whatever challenges awaited them.

Arriving at the dilapidated town, they discovered a clock tower that stood as a solitary sentinel amid the ruins. The clock's hands were frozen, its mechanism silenced by the passage of time. With careful examination, they uncovered a hidden compartment within the clock, containing an ancient parchment.

Unfurling the delicate document, they deciphered the cryptic message inscribed upon it. It revealed the location of the next clue, guiding them toward a distant mountain range that held untold mysteries within its peaks. Filled with excitement, they embarked on their next adventure, following the clues provided by the clock.

Through treacherous terrains and breathtaking vistas, they traversed the towering mountains, scaling rocky cliffs and navigating treacherous ravines.

Along the way, they encountered tests of courage and strength, outwitting cunning traps and facing formidable adversaries. Yet, their unwavering determination and the bond forged between them carried them through each obstacle. At last, standing atop the highest peak, they gazed upon a breathtaking sight—a hidden valley nestled amidst the jagged mountains.

Within its depths lay the next clue, awaiting their discovery. With bated breath and hearts full of anticipation, they ventured into the mysterious valley, ready to unravel the secrets that lay within. For they knew that their journey had only just begun, and with every clue they unveiled, they drew closer to the legendary Wild West treasure that had captivated their souls.

**And so, united by their shared purpose and strengthened by their previous triumphs, Lisa, Emma, Emily, Mia, Sophia, Sam, and Peter pressed onward. They would face the unknown, conquer their fears, and continue to unravel the enigmatic puzzle that would lead them to the ultimate treasure they sought.**

# 13. TIME TRAVEL ADVENTURE

As Lisa, Emma, Emily, Sophia, Sam, and Peter delved deeper into the mysterious valley, they came across an ancient chamber hidden beneath a towering waterfall. Inside, they discovered a remarkable contraption—an intricately crafted time travel machine.

Amidst their awe and wonder, they realized that this machine held the power to transport them through time, opening up a whole new realm of possibilities in their quest.

Excitement surged through their veins as they contemplated the adventures and discoveries that awaited them.

With a mix of anticipation and trepidation, they activated the time travel machine. Its gears creaked into motion, emitting a soft hum as it harnessed the energies of the universe. A swirling vortex appeared before them, a gateway to the unknown.

One by one, they stepped into the shimmering portal, their bodies tingling with the sensation of time and space bending around them.

**The world around them transformed as they were whisked away on a journey through the annals of history**

**As Lisa, Emma, Emily, Sophia, Sam, and Peter stepped through the swirling vortex, they felt a disorienting shift in their surroundings. The familiar landscape of the mysterious valley vanished, replaced by a new setting that seemed to defy the boundaries of time.**

**They found themselves in a bustling city, with towering skyscrapers and futuristic technology.**

**They had been transported to a time far into the future, where advanced civilizations thrived and possibilities were endless.**

**Eager to explore this brave new world, the group ventured out into the city.**

**They marveled at the sleek hovercrafts whizzing by, holographic displays showcasing breathtaking vistas, and the seamless integration of technology into everyday life.**

**It was a dazzling sight, one that made them feel like explorers in a realm beyond their wildest imaginations.**

**Guided by their insatiable curiosity, they sought out knowledge and wisdom from the inhabitants of this future society.**

**They engaged in conversations with scientists, philosophers, and artists, absorbing insights and ideas that challenged their preconceived notions of what was possible.**

**But as they delved deeper into this futuristic realm, they became aware of a troubling truth.**

**The world they had entered was not without its own set of challenges and conflicts. While technological advancements had brought prosperity, there were also disparities and social unrest that they had not anticipated.**

**The group realized that their journey through time was not just about the pursuit of treasure but also about understanding the intricacies of the human condition across different eras.**

They saw firsthand the importance of empathy, compassion, and the power of unity in shaping a better future. Motivated by this newfound realization, they resolved to use their time travel abilities to make a positive impact.

They visited different time periods, witnessing historical events and lending a helping hand where they could.

Whether it was providing aid during natural disasters, standing up against injustice, or inspiring others with their tales of adventure and resilience, they became catalysts for positive change.

However, amidst their noble endeavors, they encountered a formidable adversary.

A time-traveling villain, envious of their abilities and determined to possess the Wild West treasure for themselves, pursued them relentlessly across the ages.

They faced thrilling chases through ancient ruins, perilous encounters in war-torn landscapes, and mind-bending confrontations in parallel dimensions.

Throughout their epic battles, they relied on their unwavering camaraderie and the lessons they had learned from their diverse journeys.

Each member of the group had grown stronger and wiser, developing unique skills and perspectives that complemented one another.

Their unity became their greatest weapon against the forces that sought to disrupt the fabric of time.

As their journey neared its climax, the group came to a startling realization.

The Wild West treasure they had sought was not just a physical bounty but a symbol of the intangible riches they had discovered along the way—the bonds of friendship, the resilience of the human spirit, and the power of collective action.

With renewed purpose, they set out on their final quest—to confront the time-traveling villain, protect the Wild West treasure, and ensure that the lessons they had learned would shape a brighter future for all.

**The ultimate showdown awaited them, where they would put their newfound strengths to the test and face their greatest challenge yet.**

## 14. LOST MIA

As the group materialized in a bustling marketplace of ancient Egypt, the scorching sun beat down upon them. They marveled at the grandeur of towering pyramids and the majesty of Pharaohs and their subjects.

The air was thick with the scent of spices, and the sounds of merchants haggling filled their ears.

However, amidst their excitement, they realized that Mia was missing. Panic surged through their hearts as they searched desperately for their friend, calling out her name amidst the cacophony of the bustling city. But Mia was nowhere to be found.

In their hearts, they knew that they couldn't stay in ancient Egypt for long. Time was an elusive force, and they had to find a way to retrieve Mia and continue their journey. Determined, they vowed to leave no stone unturned, sparing no effort to reunite with their lost companion.

They combed through the bustling streets, seeking guidance from wise sages and ancient texts, hoping to unravel the mystery that had separated them from Mia. Their quest led them to a wise and aged scholar, who spoke of an ancient artifact—a powerful amulet capable of altering the fabric of time.

Driven by hope, they embarked on a perilous adventure, traversing treacherous tombs and avoiding ancient traps in their quest for the mythical amulet.

The journey tested their resolve and pushed them to their limits, but they never wavered in their determination to find Mia and bring her back to their fold.

Finally, after countless trials and tribulations, they stood before the resting place of the amulet. Its golden glow emanated an aura of power and mystique. With caution, they secured the amulet, its weight heavy in their hands, and its potential immense.

Returning to the bustling city, they focused their energies on harnessing the amulet's power. With a collective prayer, they invoked its ancient magic, beseeching it to guide them back to the moment when Mia had vanished.

As the amulet's power surged through them, a blinding light enveloped their beings, and the fabric of time warped and twisted. When the light subsided, they found themselves back in the very moment they had lost Mia, just before stepping into the time travel machine.

This time, they acted swiftly and decisively. With unwavering resolve, they ensured that Mia remained by their side as they stepped through the portal once again. Mia's presence filled them with a sense of relief and renewed purpose as they embarked on the next phase of their extraordinary journey.

And so, as they left behind the ancient wonders of Egypt, their hearts filled with the anticipation of what lay ahead. The time travel machine hummed with possibilities, carrying them to new realms and uncharted territories.

They were bound by friendship, driven by a shared purpose, and ready to face whatever challenges awaited them in the ever-unfolding tapestry of time.

# 15.ANCIENT EGYPT

**As Lisa, Emma, Emily, Sophia, Sam, Mia, and Peter stepped through the portal of the time travel machine once again, they were greeted by a kaleidoscope of sights, sounds, and sensations.**

**The landscape shifted and transformed around them, as they were transported to a realm unlike anything they had ever encountered before.**

**They found themselves in a world where the boundaries of time and space intertwined, where past, present, and future coexisted in a mesmerizing tapestry of existence. They stood on the precipice of infinite possibilities, ready to embark on a journey that transcended the confines of conventional reality.**

**Guided by their insatiable curiosity and their unbreakable bond, the group ventured forth into this extraordinary realm. They witnessed the rise and fall of civilizations, traversed ancient landscapes brimming with myth and legend, and encountered beings of both extraordinary power and profound wisdom.**

With each passing era, they absorbed the wisdom and experiences offered by the inhabitants of these temporal realms. They learned from ancient philosophers, fought alongside legendary warriors, and conversed with scholars and visionaries whose ideas shaped the course of history.

Yet, amidst the breathtaking wonders and the profound knowledge they acquired, they also faced their fair share of trials and tribulations. They encountered dark forces that sought to disrupt the delicate fabric of time, threatening to unleash chaos and destruction upon the realms they visited.

As their journeys carried them from one era to another, they encountered formidable adversaries who wielded ancient magic, advanced technology, or a combination of both. But through their unwavering unity, resourcefulness, and indomitable spirit, they overcame every challenge that stood in their path.

Throughout their adventures, they discovered hidden clues and cryptic messages that hinted at the ultimate purpose of their quest. They realized that their journey through time was not just a grand adventure or a search for treasure, but a quest to restore balance and harmony to the very fabric of existence.

The answers they sought were not contained in a physical artifact or a singular destination. Instead, the true treasure lay within themselves—their collective wisdom, their boundless compassion, and their unwavering belief in the power of unity and love.

In their final confrontation, they faced the embodiment of the forces that sought to unravel the tapestry of time. It was a battle that transcended mere physical combat, as they relied on their profound understanding of the interconnectedness of all things to overcome their adversary.

Through a fusion of ancient wisdom, futuristic technology, and the strength of their unbreakable bond, they emerged triumphant. The balance was restored, and the realms they had visited were once again in harmony.

As the time travel machine hummed with a final surge of energy, the group found themselves back in the present, their minds and hearts forever transformed by the incredible journey they had undertaken.

They stood together, their spirits soaring with a profound sense of purpose and the knowledge that their adventures were far from over. The realms of time and space beckoned, offering limitless possibilities and untold mysteries waiting to be unraveled.

And so, with their spirits aflame and their hearts united, Lisa, Emma, Emily, Sophia, Sam, Mia, and Peter prepared to embark on a new chapter of their extraordinary journey.

With the tapestry of time as their guide and the power of their collective will, they would continue to explore, to learn, and to make their mark upon the ever-unfolding story of existence.

The next part of their story was about to begin, and its pages were filled with the promise of unimaginable wonders and boundless adventures. The group stood ready to face the challenges, embrace the unknown, and forever leave their mark on the tapestry of time

As Lisa, Emma, Emily, Sophia, Sam, Mia, and Peter prepared for the next phase of their extraordinary journey, they couldn't help but feel a mix of excitement and trepidation.

They had triumphed over numerous challenges, unraveled the mysteries of different eras, and forged unbreakable bonds along the way. But the path ahead was still shrouded in uncertainty, and the true nature of their quest remained elusive.

With their time travel machine fully charged and their spirits ablaze with anticipation, the group set their sights on a new destination.

They input the coordinates into the machine, its gears whirring and lights flickering as it prepared to transport them once again.

As the familiar hum filled the air, the group felt a surge of energy enveloping them, transporting them beyond the constraints of time and space.

They emerged in a land veiled in mist—a realm of myth and legend, where magic crackled in the air and ancient secrets lay dormant, waiting to be uncovered.

They had arrived in the realm of Avalon, a place steeped in Arthurian legend and enchantment. Towering castles rose against a backdrop of lush greenery, and knights clad in shining armor roamed the land. It was a realm where chivalry and honor held sway, and the echoes of ancient prophecies whispered through the winds.

Drawn by an unseen force, the group ventured deeper into the heart of Avalon. They sought guidance from wise sorceresses, consulted ancient tomes, and deciphered cryptic riddles that led them closer to the truth. Along the way, they encountered mythical creatures, battled malevolent sorcerers, and encountered knights of both noble and treacherous intent.

Through their trials and triumphs, they unearthed fragments of a forgotten prophecy—a prophecy that spoke of a great cosmic event that would shape the destiny of all realms.

The answer to their ultimate quest lay in unraveling the mysteries of this prophecy and understanding their role in the unfolding cosmic tapestry.

As they delved deeper into the heart of Avalon, the group discovered a hidden sanctuary—a sacred grove imbued with ancient magic. It was said to be the dwelling place of the mythical Lady of the Lake, the guardian of profound wisdom and the key to unlocking the secrets of the prophecy.

In a solemn ceremony, guided by the words of an ancient incantation, the Lady of the Lake appeared before them—a radiant figure shrouded in ethereal mist. With eyes filled with both sorrow and hope, she shared the missing pieces of the prophecy, revealing their true purpose and the vital role they played in preserving the delicate balance of all realms.

The group learned that the great cosmic event, foretold in the prophecy, was drawing near—an event that would test their strength, resolve, and unwavering belief in the power of unity. They were chosen as the guardians of the realms, tasked with preventing an imminent catastrophe and restoring harmony to the cosmic tapestry.

Armed with newfound knowledge and a sense of purpose that burned brighter than ever, Lisa, Emma, Emily, Sophia, Sam, Mia, and Peter embraced their destiny. They would travel across realms, unite ancient allies, and confront formidable adversaries to fulfill their role as guardians. The path ahead was fraught with danger and uncertainty, but they faced it with unyielding courage and the unshakeable bond that had grown between them. As they embarked on the next chapter of their journey, they knew that the fate of all realms hung in the balance—and their actions would determine the course of the ever-unfolding story. With the power of time and the wisdom of Avalon on their side, they set forth, ready to face whatever challenges lay ahead. The cosmic tapestry awaited their touch, and the threads of destiny weaved their way through their intertwined lives. And now they visit the king of the ancient Egypt. They was shocked that how the king was know them and not only them he know that cave monster and all the adventure that we do. How? Who was this king? How he know them? But don't worry next part coming soon.

-The End-

**The Next Part is Coming Soon........**

## About Next Part :

As Lisa, Emma, Emily, Mia, Sophia, Sam, and Peter continued their journey through time, they knew that each step brought them closer to the legendary treasure. The adventures they had encountered had forged unbreakable bonds, and their resolve to uncover the secrets of the Wild West remained unyielding. Their path would take them to uncharted territories, ancient civilizations, and perhaps even into the unknown reaches of the cosmos. They were prepared to confront new challenges, engage in epic battles, and unravel the deepest mysteries that time had to offer. Stay tuned for the next chapter of their extraordinary journey, where they would face ancient gods, mythical creatures, and the timeless allure of the Wild West treasure. Together, they would leave an indelible mark on history and etch their names among the legends of the ages.

As Lisa, Emma, Emily, Mia, Sophia, Sam, and Peter pressed forward, their hearts brimming with anticipation, they found themselves transported to a realm of celestial wonders. They stood atop a mountain peak, surrounded by a breathtaking expanse of stars and galaxies. It was a place where time itself seemed to stand still, and the mysteries of the universe unfolded before their eyes.

In this ethereal realm, they encountered beings of immense wisdom and power—celestial guardians who held the keys to unlocking the secrets of the Wild West treasure. These celestial guides shared ancient prophecies and bestowed upon them enchanted artifacts, imbued with cosmic energies t

hat would aid them in their quest.

With their newfound cosmic companions, the group embarked on a journey through the stars. They traversed galaxies, encountered celestial anomalies, and braved the unknown in their pursuit of the Wild West treasure. Each planet they visited revealed a clue, a fragment of the grand puzzle that would lead them closer to their ultimate goal.

Throughout their cosmic odyssey, they faced trials that tested not only their physical prowess but also their inner strength and unwavering determination. They confronted cosmic storms, navigated treacherous asteroid fields, and even ventured into the heart of a black hole, where the very fabric of reality threatened to unravel.

But through their unity and unwavering resolve, they emerged victorious, each trial strengthening their bonds and deepening their understanding of the true meaning of their quest. Along the way, they encountered beings from other realms and civilizations, forging alliances and learning from their diverse perspectives.

As they ventured deeper into the cosmos, a sense of awe and reverence filled their souls. They realized that the Wild West treasure was not just a physical bounty but a symbol of knowledge, wisdom, and the untamed spirit of adventure that resided within each of them.

Finally, after traversing countless light-years and unlocking the last cosmic gate, they stood at the precipice of a magnificent nebula—a breathtaking tapestry of colors and energies. The nebula revealed the location of the Wild West treasure, concealed within a distant star system.

But as they prepared to embark on their final leg of the journey, they faced their most heartbreaking moment yet. Mia, their dear friend, who had journeyed with them through time and space, revealed that she could go no further. Her purpose in the quest had been fulfilled, and her destiny lay in a different realm.

With heavy hearts, they bid Mia farewell, knowing that her presence would forever be etched in their memories. They honored her sacrifice and vowed to continue the quest in her honor, knowing that her spirit would guide them from afar. And so, with renewed determination and a profound sense of purpose, Lisa, Emma, Emily, Sophia, Sam, and Peter set their course for the distant star system. The final frontier awaited them, and the Wild West treasure beckoned.

As they sailed through the cosmos, the stars themselves seemed to cheer them on, twinkling with anticipation. They were not alone in their pursuit—legends and heroes of the past whispered their support, and the cosmic forces aligned in their favor.

What trials and wonders awaited them in the star system? What guardians would stand in their way, testing their mettle one final time? The answers lay ahead, as their grand adventure approached its climax.

Stay tuned for the thrilling conclusion of their epic journey, where the destiny of the Wild West treasure and the fate of all realms would be decided. The stage was set for an unforgettable finale, where the true nature of their quest would be revealed and the legacy they would leave behind would be written in the stars....

# Surprising Gift

**Write your own small story about the next part and send me on my whatsapp 9422174811....... The <u>surprising gift is waiting for you......</u>**

**Your Story ( Minimum 1000 words) : ---------------**

--------------------------------------------------

--------------------------------------------------

--------------------------------------------------

--------------------------------------------------

--------------------------------------------------

--------------------------------------------------

--------------------------------------------------

--------------------------------------------------

--------------------------------------------------

--------------------------------------------------

--------------------------------------------------

--------------------------------------------------

--------------------------------------------------

--------------------------------------------------

--------------------------------------------------

--------------------------------------------------

--------------------------------------------------

--------------------------------------------------

--------------------------------------------------

-----------------------------------------------------

-----------------------------------------------------

-----------------------------------------------------

-----------------------------------------------------

-----------------------------------------------------

-----------------------------------------------------

-----------------------------------------------------

-----------------------------------------------------

-----------------------------------------------------

-----------------------------------------------------

-----------------------------------------------------

-----------------------------------------------------

-----------------------------------------------------

------

**Your Name** :
**Age** :
**Country Name** :
**State Name** :

# THANK YOU

www.ingramcontent.com/pod-product-compliance
Lightning Source LLC
LaVergne TN
LVHW021144160826
845679LV00023B/2032

* 9 7 9 8 8 9 1 3 3 4 8 2 3 *